CHANDRAHASA

THE WAR BEGINS

RUDRAKSH MISHRA

Made with ❤ on the Notion Press Platform
www.notionpress.com

Contents

Contents

CONNECT WITH AUTHOR

Instagram- author_rudraksh

Preface

In the epic tale of 'Chandrahasa: The Sword of Destiny,' a mystical and powerful sword called Chandrahasa takes center stage. Chandrahasa, once the revered commander of an army in the kingdom of hell, holds the spirit of its fearless leader. Tragedy befalls the kingdom when a war between the king and prince weakens their paradise, leading to foreign invasions and the eventual defeat of Chandrahasa's army.

Chandrahasa and a fragment of his surviving army find shelter in a distant world offered by the compassionate rulers of a different realm. However, their newfound sanctuary is soon threatened as a coalition of kingdoms launches a relentless invasion, resulting in the army's defeat. In a final act of sacrifice, Chandrahasa leaves his mortal body and entrusts his soul to the royal sword of King Pulastya, the monarch of the Rudraksham kingdom.

Bound by their loyalty to Chandrahasa, his devoted army pledges their allegiance to the bloodline of Pulastya, vowing to follow their commands forever. Pulastya, determined to preserve the legacy of Chandrahasa, constructs a dedicated palace to house the sacred sword.

2Meanwhile, a dynamic array of gods, goddesses, and powerful rulers from various realms emerges, each with their own unique abilities and agendas. The God of air, Rudraksha, rules with aggression and conquest, expanding his kingdom of Rudraksham to encompass not only his own planet but also numerous planets across different universes. His insatiable thirst for power leads him to challenge gods and overthrow kings, bringing turmoil to the 28 hells themselves.

Amidst the chaos, Agastya III, the God of dark energy, rises as a beacon of peace and spirituality. With a focus on non-war policies, Agastya III seeks to bring harmony to his kingdom and maintain a delicate balance amidst the growing conflicts.

As the story unfolds, it delves into the intricate web of alliances, rivalries, and cosmic battles that shape the destiny of these extraordinary characters. With the sword Chandrahasa, the charismatic Geame the Marcowich, the goddess Felicity, the land god Hemsmen, the military general Serik, and a host of other captivating characters, 'Chandrahasa: The Sword of Destiny' weaves a mesmerizing tale of power, sacrifice, and the eternal struggle between darkness and light.'

Acknowledgements

AUTHOR:

Rudraksh Mishra, born on 6th of December 2007, calls Lucknow his hometown and with this Lucknow's inquisitive nature into his personal account implicates against his peer world globally. His passion to know is what directs him to explore and find his life's secrets on his own . He is immensely driven to find the reasons and the hows, that lurk beyond the surface of the things around him. Thus, the endless bouts of unconventional inquiries that he did experience molded him in such a way that he could author multiform stories with distinct perspectives.

Interestingly enough, young Rudraksh saw his passion towards writing from the young age that he could clearly recall. He not only dared to write short stories and shared them with local newspapers but also encountered the difficulties associated with it. With the passage time, his works found their way in local publications which anchored him to the community he lived in and opened him up as a person receiving appreciation from local audience. Against the underlying truth of the conventional wisdom for a 13-year-old, Rudraksh worked to prove the skeptics wrong through his captivating articles exploring the noteworthy concept of parrallel worlds being publicized on the international spectrum, which led to his significant popularity.

Specializing in fiction, Rudraksh penning is worth noting

because of his amusing stories using which he carries the readers to new heights, full of infinite possibilities. Alongside his beautiful prose, his poetry holds more stirring thoughts that portray the dimension of ultra-modern society, and these ideas give an insight on how the world works. The fact that the news publications of all these eminent media houses have paid attention to his performance both inside and outside of the Indian territory has made more and more audiences throng to him.

Despite having only just begun his writing journey, Rudraksh is already an accomplished young writer whose previous articles like "The Lost Friend" and "The Secret Existence" prove that he is a powerful and unique talent yet to join the literary elite and create the works that will be known and respected by the world.

Prologue

Characters:

Pulastya:

Background: Pulastya is the king of the Rudraksham kingdom and the father of Rudraksha. He holds a significant position as the ruler of his realm. Only the royal family of the Agastyam kingdom, who share the same lineage as the Rudraksham kingdom, has the authority to command Chandrahasa, the Sword. Pulastya's devotion to preserving the sword's power is evident in the construction of a dedicated palace where Chandrahasa is kept.

Role: Pulastya plays a vital role in safeguarding the legacy of Chandrahasa and ensuring that its command remains within the chosen bloodline. As the king, he holds authority and responsibility over his kingdom and its people.

Rudraksha:

Background: Rudraksha is the God of air, possessing a unique ability to dominate all the natural kingdoms (Air, Fire, Land, Water, Soul) when facing a combination of grief and anger. He is the successor of King Pulastya and the youngest child of the king. Rudraksha is not only a great scholar but also a devoted follower of Lord Shiva.

Personality: Rudraksha is an aggressive and ambitious king. During his reign, his kingdom of Rudraksham became the most powerful in existence. He was constantly driven to conquer, expanding his rule beyond his own planet to invade numerous planets across various universes. Rudraksha's thirst for power and knowledge led him to dethrone gods and kings of the 28 hells, showcasing his incredible might.

Abilities: Rudraksha is nearly immortal, with the exception of being susceptible to assassination through a special bow called "Palintonos." He possesses vast knowledge of wormholes, enabling him to travel through them and explore different realms and universes within a matter of hours.

Agastya III:

Background: Agastya III is the successor of the Agastyam kingdom. Unlike his aggressive counterparts, he follows a policy of non-war, prioritizing peace and spirituality. He is known for his deep spirituality and a strong inclination towards peace. Agastya III upholds the traditions and values set by his ancestors in the Agastyam kingdom.

Personality: Agastya III is a peace-loving king who seeks spiritual enlightenment. He is wise and compassionate, focusing on maintaining harmony within his kingdom and promoting peaceful coexistence with other realms and civilizations.

Suryahasa:

Background: Suryahasa is the grandson of Chandrahasa, the powerful commander whose spirit resides in the royal sword. As a member of the royal bloodline, Suryahasa inherits the loyalty of Chandrahasa's army, who vowed to follow the commands of their commander forever.

Geame The Marcowich:

Background: Geame is the Prince of the Marcowich kingdom and the god of the fire kingdom. He hails from the planet Alexeria and arrives on Earth with a vast army. Despite his immense power, Geame is known for his fair and just rule. He has never been cruel to the civilians of any kingdom he has invaded. Earth falls under his dominion, and his kingdom is so formidable that no other kingdom can even penetrate the protective boundaries of the Marcowich kingdom.

Personality: Geame is a powerful and respected leader. While he possesses great strength, he also demonstrates wisdom and restraint in his actions. He governs his kingdom with fairness and ensures the well-being of his subjects. Geame's presence and rule make him a formidable force within the story.

Abilities: Geame possesses an innate control over the element of fire, enabling him to wield its destructive power with unparalleled mastery. His abilities extend to summoning and manipulating flames on an unprecedented scale, making him a fearsome force on the battlefield.

Tactics: Geame's strategic brilliance is widely acknowledged. He possesses a tactical mind that allows him to anticipate his enemies' moves and devise intricate battle plans. Combined with his overwhelming firepower, this makes him a formidable adversary to any opposing force.

Felicity:

Background: Felicity is the Goddess of spirits and the elder sister of Geame the Marcowich. She holds a significant divine status and possesses the ability to connect with and manipulate spirits. Her role as a goddess grants her immense influence and power.

Hemsmen:

Background: Hemsmen is the spouse of Felicity and holds the title of the God of the land kingdom. He governs and protects the realm associated with land and its resources. As a divine being, Hemsmen possesses unique abilities and responsibilities related to the land.

Marfel Da Mashrafe:

Background: Marfel Da Mashrafe is the powerful King of Kepler-62 F, a planet known for its aggressive nature and advanced technology. He commands a vast and highly advanced army, which has allowed him to conquer and dethrone the kings of the Gaveral and Colester kingdoms on the planet. Marfel Da Mashrafe's rule extends beyond Kepler-62 F, as his ancestors and siblings reside on the planet Alexeria. Half of Alexeria is under the rule of the Marcowich kingdom, while the other half falls under

Mashrafe's control.

Personality: Marfel Da Mashrafe is known for his aggressive and assertive nature. He is a formidable leader who possesses strategic skills and utilizes advanced military technology to maintain and expand his dominion. His ambition and thirst for power drive his actions and decisions.

Challenge: The head priest of the Gaveral kingdom, known as one of the most knowledgeable priests in the universe, has empowered himself to near-immortality. However, the only being capable of defeating him is Agastya III, the God of dark energy himself.

Serik:

Background: Serik is the military general of the Mashrafe kingdom on the planet Kepler-62 F. As the general, he holds a crucial position in Marfel Da Mashrafe's army and plays a significant role in the defense and expansion of the kingdom. Serik is a skilled and experienced military leader, known for his strategic prowess and loyalty to the king.

Personality: Serik is disciplined, dedicated, and fiercely loyal to Marfel Da Mashrafe. He is a seasoned military tactician, always seeking ways to strengthen and improve the kingdom's military capabilities. Serik is known for his unwavering commitment to his duties and is highly respected by the soldiers under his command.

1

The Terminal War

"It's revenge time!" said Rudraksha. King Pulastya had two children Atharva the elder one and Rudraksha the younger one, Atharva was to be the next king. Atharva was like an antonym of Rudraksha, they were so different, their nature, their way of ruling, their prospective, their approach towards a problem. Atharva and Agastya III were very similar nobody thought Rudraksham could dominate not only their planet as well as other planets in other universes but destiny had some other plans, Atharva eventually died in an accident. His death broke king Pulastya, king Pulastya was never the same after his elder son's death. After Atharva's death Rudraksh was considered to become the king.

Chandrahasa was the commander of the army of Nostalgia kingdom in a dimension of hell. He was very loyal to his kingdom, he was very powerful despite being the ultimate power in the army he was very polite and kind to everyone. The Prince of Nostalgia kingdom wanted to be the king of the kingdom but his father was still the king. The royal family of Nostalgia often had arguments over the throne, which was affecting the whole kingdom negatively.

The prince was desperately into the wish to get the throne anyhow, this made him shake hands with his neighbour kingdoms to kill his father, the kingdom was not ready for this invasion. The prince himself was not ready, as he made a pact to only murder his father but the neighbour kingdom had other plans.

The king of the neighbour planet sent a message to the allied kingdoms of theirs, it was to combine and attack nostalgia. As per the pact only that kingdom was supposed to attack so the king at first sent a weak army to attack nostalgia so that he can win the full support of the prince by showing that he is going as per the pact. The first stage of war stretched for two weeks Nostalgia was winning, now the evil plan that was made between neighbourhood kingdoms, a big combined attack from five kingdom was no far, but Nostalgia kingdom was not ready even not the prince. The armies of all the kingdoms were over the thundering sky of Nostalgia kingdom, Chandrahasa sensed the danger he immediately sent help messages through his messengers in various directions, to various kingdoms in various worlds. One of his messengers arrived at the gates of mesmerising Rudraksham kingdom. That time Pulastya was the king, being a wise king of such powerful kingdom he immediately declared that Rudraksham will be helping Nostalgia kingdom. The armies got alarmed up, spaceships were filled up. Rudraksham kingdom helped Nostalgia kingdom to their level best but it was not up to the mark.

Pulastya knew the value of Chandrahasa, how powerful and intellectual he was, when it seemed clear that Nostalgia kingdom would be on the losing side and their kingdom would be destroyed, he ordered the military officials to immediately bring Chandrahasa back to Rudraksha kingdom safely. Chandrahasa was not ready, military officials were requesting him, he was not ready until he saw his main officers brutally injured, their family crying and begging for life this gave him a sudden shock. For the sake of his officers and their family he agreed to come with them to Rudraksha kingdom but only on one condition that he would only come if the main officers of his army would be also taken. The military officials of Rudraksham kingdom accepted his condition and took Chandrahasa along with his main army to Rudraksham kingdom.

"What a place!" an officer exclaimed. Chandrahasa touched the auspicious land of Rudraksham kingdom along with his army, they were amazed seeing the Rudraksham kingdom. King Pulastya himself welcomed Chandrahasa to his palace. That day Rudraksha met Chandrahasa for the first time, Chandrahasa was very impressed by Rudraksha. Rudraksha was about twelve years old at that time, years passed by, bond between Chandrahasa and Rudraksha got stronger. Rudraksha learned some of his most deadly war techniques from Chandrahasa. Chandrahasa used to observe Rudraksha keenly, his mindset, his physique development, his wil to be at the top, once while walking king Pulastya he ironically said that Rudraksha will become the most powerful not in just one planet, he will be the most powerful in the whole universe.

Years passed, then came the day when Chandrahasa willingly left his body and rested his spirit in the sword of king Pulastya. Pulastya was now in a state of dethroning himself and making the prince the king, "Rudraksha the king of Rudraksham". This was made up a sensational news by some courtiers who were against this decision. They debated that Rudraksha was still not ready to take the responsibility. Pulastya made the final decision to make Rudraksha the king. The decision to make Rudraksha was the turning point. The Chandrahasa sword was in a special palace built by Pulastya, after Pulastya and Virinchi (the king of Agastyam kingdom before Agastya III) only Rudraksha and Agastya III were able to use the sword.

It's time

" It's revenge time" the first words that came out of Rudraksha's mouth after his coronation, the crowd got goose bumps, they were spell bound by the kind of coronation speech Rudraksha delivered. The public of Rudraksham kingdom started chanting Rudraksha... Rudraaaksha. Rudraksha..Rudrakshaaa, seeing the reaction of the public the ministers who were against Rudraksha got their asses burned. The same night Rudraksha arranged a meeting with Agastya III. The ministers tried a lot to get what is going inside but they could not get even air of that. The meeting was long, after five hours finally the door opened and Rudraksha was walking out, he seemed furious, walking quickly in a frustrated way like he was fed up from something.

Soon Agastya III also came out, everyone was waiting for him to get what happened inside because no one was having courage to ask Rudraksha. Agastya III seemed disgraced, as everyone was asking him he just spoke one line " It's Rudraksha's time " after hearing this no-one uttered a single word, people shocked and were confused, they stood still for minutes with their jaws hanging and eyeballs moving left-right, here-there in quick sessions. " Is there any problem-solving discussion going on?" King Rudraksha asked the ministers in an ironical way. " This 16ft man with those soul-deadly arms is like a nightmare for us" a minister said to his fellow minister while walking back to their palaces.

Rudraksha was seemed very suspicious in recent nights to ministers. "Every night our Lord goes to Chandrahasa palace and stays there for hours and then come back" a minister to his wife. Chandrahasa palace is the palace where Pulastya kept Chandrahasa sword. "Is he able to contact Chandrahsa?" minister to his wife, "Maybe you are thinking too much" his wife tried to end the topic. Rudraksha was doing a meeting with Agastya III, Suryahasa (grandson of Chandrahasa) and other very special courtiers, this made people curious, everyone started making their own assumptions and spreading that, no one knew the real reason but everyone knew something they have been told by someone who also don't know anything true.

The truth behind Rudraksha's nightly visits to Chandrahasa's palace remained a mystery to the ministers and the public. Speculations and rumors started circulating, creating an air of curiosity and intrigue. Some believed that Rudraksha was able to communicate with the spirit of Chandrahasa, seeking guidance and wisdom from the powerful commander. Others thought he was secretly training with the legendary sword, honing his skills and preparing for battles to come.

Meanwhile, the kingdom of Rudraksham thrived under Rudraksha's reign. His aggressive and ambitious nature propelled the kingdom to new heights. Rudraksha was relentless in expanding his rule, not content with conquering just his own planet. His thirst for power led him to invade other planets in different universes, leaving a trail of defeated kingdoms in his wake.

With each conquest, Rudraksha's reputation grew, and his enemies trembled at the mention of his name. He became known as a formidable warrior, capable of dominating the natural kingdoms of Air, Fire, Land, Water, and even the Soul itself when consumed by grief and anger. The people of Rudraksham kingdom hailed him as a fearless and mighty ruler, their chants of "Rudraksha... Rudraaa... ksha" echoing through the streets.

But amidst the triumphs and glory, doubts and suspicions lingered among some ministers. They questioned the extent of Rudraksha's power and his true intentions. They observed his intense focus and the aura of mystery surrounding his actions. Whispers of concern filled the corridors of the palace, as they wondered if Rudraksha's pursuit of revenge and power would lead them down a dangerous path. The sword, now resting in its dedicated palace, served as a symbol of their alliance and a source of strength for Rudraksha.

As the story unfolded, the ministers and the people would come to understand the weight of Rudraksha's burden and the choices he would make in the pursuit of his goals. The path to revenge and ultimate power was paved with challenges and sacrifices, and the fate of the kingdom would be shaped by the actions of its enigmatic king.

Fear in eyes

Rudraksha, a person from whom everyone feared, he was very powerful. The public of the kingdom as well as the ministers were very curious that why he goes in the Chandrahasa palace and stays there hours and hours. This became a sensation in no time, the news travelled the universe from person to person, place to place, galaxy to galaxy. This news put neighbour kings in curiosity too, everyone knew how strong was the bond between Rudraksha and Chandrahasa, they knew how knowledgeable Rudraksha was. The ministers forced themselves to take this normally but they were helpless, they went through sleepless nights just wondering what was Rudraksha trying to do. Days passed, curiosity in the whole kingdom, seeing their irregular in assembly was the trigger for them to enquire about that on a higher level. Small groups of people along with their particular leader started gathering outside the palace of Rudraksha. The guards of the palace did not allowed them to protest or practice violence in-front of the palace, conflicts between groups and guards became serious.

Rudraksha was still absent in the assembly, seeing this public got angry, they felt their insult. Soon more people made their group to protest. The carelessness of Rudraksha led a to civil war, as the people who were in support of Rudraksha also gathered at the palace. The ministers who were against Rudraksha realised that this was an opportunity to destroy the image of Rudraksha in hearts of the public. They created a propaganda against

Rudraksha, the ministers targeted the emotions of the public. The ministers planned a well executive programme for promoting their propaganda. They wanted people to believe that Rudraksha was not following his father's Pulastya's legacy, they were executing influential programs to make people believe that Rudraksha was not an ideal king. The ministers were almost successful in the mission, the people were very disappointed from Rudraksha.

The protests were becoming vigorous day by day, the ministers were campaigning, civil wars was devastating the harmony of cities. Rudraksha was aware of everything when he realised that situation will get even worse he made an announcement that he would be there in the assembly the next day. Reading this everyone even the ministers became silent, cancelled their campaign plans, people were now even more curious. On the day of arrival of Rudraksha in the assembly, huge crowd gathered there since morning. Agastya III was also supposed to come along with his brother Rudraksha, everyone was eagerly waiting for their king. The royal cart of Rudraksha was in the main palace, Rudraksha was about to leave, Agastya III was there too, they left the palace in their royal cart. Their royal cart was like super car if we look as per our world. The public was pushing each other to sneak the arrival of Lord Rudraksha .

Rudraksha's royal cart stopped in-front of the gate of assembly, guard rushed and opened the door, the destroyer, the man himself King Rudraksha arrived in style as usual along with Agastya III. Public went crazy, forgot the protests they were doing everyone chanting " Rudraksha..... Rudra..... ture puba' kilgists Rudraksha (in the native language of Rudraksham kingdom) which means " the people's king Rudraksha" The public as well as all the courtiers were in shock. The ministers looked at each other in a shocked encounter. Rudraksha, fully armoured wearing his royal robe, walking with confidence filled steps, looking straight into the eyes of those councillors was a terrifying and shocking sight for the ministers. Everyone was surprised and confused that why was he coming with the kingdom's pride which was kept untouched from several years. As soon as he stepped on the first stair, the ministers moved to corners, in their hearts they were trembling as they were campaigning against him thinking that the public was angry at him and they will show that anger at him in the assembly but the public forgot all their anger and got influenced by the aura Rudraksha was carrying in his hands. That was an amusing sight, 16ft heavenly powered man with heart winning charm that was dripping from his personality, the aura he created, those big soul-deadly arms holding the deadly Chandrahasa sword.

The speech that Rudraksha delivered was so intense and terrifying for some people, the ministers were now sure that they were left with no option except surrendering themselves to King Rudraksha. Few months ago, just after couple of weeks Rudraksha's coronation, Rudraksha consolidated lands of various officials, richer public of the state who were having loads of black money, but at that time Rudraksha did not disclosed his intentions, as the councillors were putting this up as a propaganda, he was with no option other than to disclose the reality. He was distributing those properties in the public of the state. Rudraksha announced that he will be on a mission of conquering all the kingdoms of hell. It was way too clear that Nostalgia kingdom would be the first kingdom to be attacked by Rudraksham army.

The attacks were about to be on a go in just about two days after the speech, that was a very shocking decision taken by the King, it was hard to believe for anyone there that how could be the kingdom prepared for the war In so short time. The war declaring statement extracted from his speech is " I said it earlier, It's revenge time, revenge of the great Chandrahasa, revenge of the brutality they showed, It's Nostalgia kingdom now, I will make it Chandrahasa kingdom, they tried to kill the family of the great Chandrahasa, I will slaughter their entire bloodline, they broke the war fare rules, I will dislocate the whole hell." This made it clear to the public that what Rudraksha was about to do, but they were in support of him as they knew that their king was a very well-administrated king, he understood every circumstance of the kingdom, took harsh but right steps and this time he was about to expand the kingdom.

The councillors were now very tensed and trembling, on the very same night, they all were together, searching for a way in which they could save themselves from getting sacked, they realised that the public was with Rudraksha. "

He won the hearts again, how is he so perfect in this, wherever he goes he makes the public his devotee" a minister to the other three while discussing about the speech of Rudraksha. "Huh! He is master in this" they were sweating, they knew that Rudraksha will never leave them so easily. They were chattering about that in between that they heard someone calling their names they looked through the window. " God! Our death!! Our death, messenger from the court of Rudraksha" a courtier screamed. Glasses of wine dropped from the hands, eyes started becoming wet, heart pumping to the limit, face turned pale, frozen jaws, wet eyes, cry baby face, those courtiers were experiencing a near to death moment. The special messenger knocked the door. " calm, let's open the door, we cannot deny message from Rudraksha" a courtier said. " He is not a normal living being like us, he is ultimate supreme! We will present ourselves under his feet, he will leave us!" They were ready to do anything in favour of Rudraksha's mercy, that shows what king Rudraksha was.

The courtiers moved to their carts and started moving towards the palace, their legs were not moving in the direction of Rudraksha, somehow they reached the door of the special meeting room where king Rudraksha was, the door opened, Rudraksha sitting on the throne looking straight into the eyes of the courtiers, they froze. "Welcome my courtiers, welcome" king Rudraksha said in a loud and clear voice. The legs of the courtiers instantly moved forward, sat on their particular seat, which was fixed for the courtiers. Agastya III looked towards

Rudraksha, they both stood up. Rudraksha was moving towards them, it seemed like it is the end time for the courtiers. "Good Night" wished king Rudraksha and then moved out. It took two minutes for the courtiers to realise that he was gone, he called them up just to wish good night, but it was more like a warning, he was showing them the power he hold just in his message.

"What is he? He took our soul out just by looking in our eyes, he called just for this good night" said a courtier. " We cannot do anything, he is the supreme" The courtiers started moving back to their respective palaces. None of the courtiers slept that night, horrified, scared. The whole kingdom was tensed, that Rudraksham kingdom was going to attack in a short time and that too in a different world. The real plan was hidden, only King Rudraksha, Agastya III and Suryahasa knew the plan. Assembly was called off the next day, this made people more worried and curious. King Rudraksha called up an urgent meeting with army officials, it was the declaration of the war, everyone knew it already that the first to be attacked would be Nostalgia Kingdom, the kingdom whose army Chandrahasa used to command of.

2

In the court of Kratium Kingdom

The happenings of the Rudraksham kingdom especially the news about the war declaration spread into various lands, the news also reached one of the allies of the Kratium kingdom, the same kingdom which invaded Nostalgia kingdom. The ally kingdom quickly informed Kratium kingdom about this, this topic got a lot of attention within a couple of days. The king of Kratium kingdom along with his allies knew that they can't beat Rudraksha easily, and they were also confused about the Chandrahasa mystery.

IN THE COURT-

King Kratium VI (the king of Kratium kingdom at the time of Rudraksha) : As much as I have heard Rudraksha is one of the smartest mind in the universe, and powerful as well. Among us Kratium, Qwerty and Opel kingdom are the strongest and we cannot face the brutal war strategies of a kingdom like Rudraksham.

King Tanger III (king of Tanger kingdom): I think we need a kingdom, a big kingdom like Rudraksham kingdom by our side.

King Opel II (King of Opel Kingdom): We also need to have divine powers like Rudraksha by our side who can match toe to toe, else the game is already over for us.

King Kratium: One more thing is that we don't what is the mystery behind the Chandrahasa sword.

King Opel II: They may be powerful but we are collectively 10 kingdoms, after all Rudraksha is a young king and he is attacking on 10 kingdoms, this is not easy for him too.

King Goister (king of Goister kingdom): He is all alone but he is more powerful than most of our neighbouring kingdoms himself.

King Mizer VI (king of Mizer Kingdom): I agree with King Opel, if we unite we can trap him easily.

King kratium VI: I think we should choose safer side and seek support of someone of that level. We have to search for kingdoms who can be on our side.

King Mizer VI: I had attacked a kingdom of a different world several times, but never did a bit of damage, they humiliated my army, we could try seeking help from them.

King Kratium VI: Aren't they your enemy?

King Mizer VI: They are but I once tried to improve our relationship too so maybe and if we win then we will let them have Rudraksham Kingdom.

King Opel II: Who are they?

King Mizer VI: The name of the kingdom is Mashrafe Kingdom.

....

King Kratium VI immediately ordered his officials to send the message to Mashrafe Kingdom. The war was heating up now, both the sides were preparing for the war. No one was aware how the Chandrahasa sword works.

Meanwhile the news about the war, the coming of Chandrahasa sword leaked into the crowds. The public of Nostalgia Kingdom found their eyes wet after hearing the name "Chandrahasa". Their loyal commander who dedicated his whole life to the kingdom. Rudraksha Kingdom, the kingdom which helped Nostalgia kingdom when no one did.

The commander arrived at the court of Kratium kingdom once again with a news.

Commander: Lord Kratium VI, we found the kingdom Mashrafe, chronologically we have sent the friendship message to them. We gathered some information too.
Mashrafes are currently ruling over several planets in several universes. Their present king "Marfel Da Mashrafe" is in preparation for clashing with their one and only rival in the whole universe "The Marcowichs" once again. The Marcowichs are currently ruling over several planets in several universes.

King Kratium VI: In between them who is stronger?

Commander: Lord, according to me it is hard to conclude both are very powerful. If Mashrafe came in our support, there is a danger too. That is they can defeat all of us very easily.

King Kratium VI: That would be same as of what we did to Nostalgia kingdom. What about the other?

Commander: The Marcowichs are the only ones who can give a fight to Mashrafes.

King Kratium VI: So what if we ask help from Marcowichs?

Commander: Lord, in their case I don't think any member of the royal family would come to fight from either kingdoms, unless we poke them about their rival and pour smoke in their eyes that Mashrafes are with Rudraksha and we need their help.

King Kratium VI: Why not! The three super powerful kingdoms should clash with each other. Arrange a meeting with Marcowichs too, and tell them that the Mashrafes are our enemy.

Commander: There is one problem too.

King Kratium VI: We will see that later, we have at least two days. First try contacting.

IN THE COURT OF OPEL KINGDOM

King Opel II: They are overhyping the powers of Rudraksha,

he is just like a kid in-front of us.

King Mizer VI: He is powerful no doubt, but here he is fighting against group of kingdoms, maybe bigger kingdoms.

King Opel II: Exactly, now we have to prove them that he is not that strong all by ourselves.

King Mizer VI: How about if we surprise him by attacking him first.

King Opel II: Excellent! We will prove ourselves as the bravest.

....

The commander of Kratium Kingdom started contacting the Marcowichs, meanwhile Opel and Mizer kingdoms were preparing for a surprise attack over Rudraksham kingdom. The things started getting messed up. The Marchowichs vs The Mashrafes vs The Kratium kingdom and allies vs The Rudraksham kingdom. We all know Karma very well, king Kratium were not loyal to the prince of the Nostalgia kingdom as per their pact, karma hits everyone, one of the officials of Mizer kingdom sent the information about the secret attack king Mizer VI and Opel II were planning of. The official was loyal but for Chandrahasa.
king Mizer VI and king Opel II were not aware that they were going to face their own death on their own.

....

IN THE COURT OF RUDRAKSHAM KINGDOM
(the messenger read the message that the official sent)

Minister 1: Counter attack? When, from where? How strong are they?

Minister 2: Are they all attacking?

Minister 3: I think we should abort the war.

Rudraksha: Sorry to interrupt but I think, I am the king. (in a bold and clear voice)

Agastya III: Rudraksha, we have to make a quick decision.

Rudraksha: My dear brother, the decision is made already. Rudraksham kingdom never steps back.

....

Rudraksha and Agastya went in Rudraksha's room for some private discussion. Suryahasa was called in too. Various ministers and other officials were being called in one by one and were given some orders. The war was getting heated, everyone was everyone's enemy. No kingdom was fully aware about the kingdoms participating. Wars within a war, enemies within the kingdom, a new surprise waiting at every step, who attacks who, who conquers who. **"CHANDRAHASA: THE WAR BEGINS"**.

3

In the previous chapter we read that Kratium is trying to seek help from both Marcowich kingdom and Mashrafe kingdom. The two kingdoms which are one of the strongest kingdoms in the whole space collective of all universes. They wanted to clash with each other, and here the clash is. Well, such powerful kingdoms like them don't indulge in wars with their full potential, neither any of their royal family takes part in war generally.

MARCOWICH KINGDOM COURT
In the court of Marcowich kingdom:

King Marvik III (King of Marcowich Kingdom): My fellow council members, the situation has become quite complicated with Kratium seeking our help against Mashrafe. We must carefully consider our options before making any decisions.

Council Member 1: Your Majesty, it is true that Mashrafe and Marcowich are formidable rivals, but should we involve ourselves in this conflict?

Council Member 2: I agree. We have always maintained a neutral stance, focusing on the prosperity and stability of our own kingdom. Engaging in external wars could jeopardize our interests.

King Marvik III: I understand your concerns, but we cannot disregard the potential consequences of Mashrafe aligning with Rudraksham kingdom. It could tip the balance of power in the entire space collective. We must analyze the risks and benefits of each choice.

Council Member 3: Your Majesty, if we do choose to support Kratium, we should ensure that our involvement is limited. We can provide them with strategic advice and intelligence without committing our forces directly.

Council Member 4: Agreed. We should maintain our position as mediators, attempting to de-escalate the situation rather than actively participating in the conflict.

King Marvik III: Wise counsel, my loyal advisors. Let it be known that Marcowich kingdom will offer diplomatic support to Kratium kingdom, acting as mediators and facilitators in their negotiations with Mashrafe. We shall work towards a peaceful resolution if possible.

The decision was met with mixed reactions within the court. Some council members were relieved by the measured approach, while others expressed concerns about potential backlash from Mashrafe. Nevertheless, the path of diplomacy was chosen, and emissaries were dispatched to Kratium to convey Marcowich's intentions.

Meanwhile, in Mashrafe Kingdom, a similar discussion was taking place.

MASHRAFE KINGDOM COURT:

King Marfel Da Mashrafe (King of Mashrafe Kingdom): My esteemed advisors, we have received a request for alliance from Kratium kingdom, who is facing the threat of Rudraksham kingdom.

Advisor 1: Your Majesty, Rudraksham has proven to be a formidable force, and their alliance with Mashrafe would certainly tip the scales in their favor.

Advisor 2: It is true that we have long-standing rivalry with Marcowich kingdom, but engaging in this war may lead to unforeseen consequences. We must weigh our options carefully.

King Marfel Da Mashrafe: I understand your concerns, but we must also consider the potential benefits of aligning with Rudraksham. If they emerge victorious, our position and influence would be significantly enhanced.

Advisor 3: Your Majesty, we have to consider the stability of the space collective. Engaging in a war of this magnitude could lead to widespread chaos and unrest. We should explore diplomatic solutions instead.

King Marfel Da Mashrafe: I concur. We shall send diplomats to both Kratium and Rudraksham, expressing our willingness to negotiate a peaceful resolution. Our reputation as a fair and just kingdom must not be tarnished by unnecessary bloodshed.

With the decision made, Mashrafe kingdom sent diplomats to both Kratium and Rudraksham, offering their services as mediators in the conflict. The intention was to explore diplomatic avenues and find a way to avoid an all-out war.

As the tension escalated and the alliances shifted, the space collective found itself on the brink of a massive confrontation. The choices made by each kingdom would shape the course of the war and determine the fate of the realms involved.

4
Mid-Way

In the midst of rising tensions and the looming specter of war, the kingdoms of Kratium, Rudraksham, Marcowich, and Mashrafe found themselves at a critical juncture. The fate of the space collective hung in the balance as they contemplated their next moves.

KRATIUM KINGDOM COURT

King Kratium VI: My esteemed council members, the time has come for us to engage in diplomatic negotiations. We have received responses from both Marcowich and Mashrafe kingdoms, expressing their willingness to mediate and seek a peaceful resolution. It is imperative that we seize this opportunity.

Council Member 1: Your Majesty, how do we proceed? Should we hold separate negotiations with each kingdom, or should we convene a larger summit involving all parties?

King Kratium VI: It is an excellent question. Given the complexities of the situation, I believe a larger summit would be more beneficial. We must create an environment for open dialogue, where all concerns can be addressed and compromises can be sought.

Council Member 2: Your Majesty, what about the Chandrahasa sword? Its mystery still remains, and it could potentially be a decisive factor in the conflict.

King Kratium VI: You are correct. The Chandrahasa sword holds immense power, and we must seek to unravel its secrets. I propose that we invite Rudraksha himself to the summit, and under the supervision of neutral experts, explore the nature and capabilities of the sword.

Council Member 3: Your Majesty, should we trust Rudraksha to attend the summit? There is a risk that he may use this opportunity to gather intelligence or gain an upper hand.

King Kratium VI: Your concerns are valid. We shall implement stringent security measures and ensure the presence of our own experts to safeguard our interests. Let us extend the invitation to Rudraksha with the understanding that his attendance will be subject to our terms and conditions.

Preparations for the summit were set into motion. Diplomatic envoys were dispatched to Rudraksham, Marcowich, and Mashrafe kingdoms, formally inviting them to participate. Meanwhile, experts in ancient artifacts and mystical artifacts were called upon to study and analyze the Chandrahasa sword, uncovering its secrets.

RUDRAKSHAM KINGDOM

Rudraksha: Agastya, the time for negotiations has come. We must tread carefully and ensure the safety and interests of our kingdom.

Agastya III: Indeed, brother. The summit presents an opportunity for us to dispel misunderstandings and find a peaceful resolution. We shall attend, but only on our own terms.

Rudraksha: I agree, Agastya. We must be cautious and remain vigilant. The secrets of the Chandrahasa sword must not fall into the wrong hands.

As the summit approached, tensions remained high, but the hope for a peaceful resolution persisted. The kingdoms of Kratium, Rudraksham, Marcowich, and Mashrafe understood the gravity of the situation and the potential consequences of a full-scale war. The stage was set for a historic gathering where alliances would be tested, negotiations would be fierce, and the destiny of the space collective would be determined.

THE SUMMIT

Leaders, diplomats, and experts from the four kingdoms converged at a neutral location for the summit. The atmosphere was charged with anticipation and apprehension as discussions were about to begin.

King Kratium VI: Welcome, esteemed guests. We gather here today to seek a peaceful resolution to the conflicts that threaten our realms. Let us engage in open and honest dialogue, with the common goal of preserving peace and prosperity.

Representatives from each kingdom presented their grievances, aspirations, and proposed solutions. Debates ensued, tempers flared, and compromises were sought. Amidst the negotiations, the experts delved into the mysteries of the Chandrahasa sword, uncovering its ancient origins and its potential for both destruction and salvation. Days turned into weeks as the summit continued. It became evident that each kingdom held deep-rooted fears, ambitions, and desires that shaped their stance. The task of finding common ground seemed daunting, but the participants were committed to exploring every avenue for peace.

In the midst of the discussions, alliances shifted, new understandings were forged, and unexpected bonds began to form. The fate of the space collective hinged on the outcome of these deliberations, and the leaders knew that a single misstep could plunge them into irreversible conflict.

5

The Demand

The summit had reached a critical stage, with the kingdoms of Kratium, Rudraksham, Marcowich, and Mashrafe inching closer to a peaceful solution. However, hidden motives and personal ambitions threatened to derail the progress made so far.

Within the council chambers, tensions ran high as King Mizer VI of Mizer Kingdom and King Opel II of Opel Kingdom voiced their demands. Their eyes gleamed with a sinister determination as they stared at the enigmatic Chandrahasa sword, now on display before them.

King Mizer VI: Rudraksha, we demand control over the Chandrahasa sword. Its power must be harnessed for the greater good of our collective kingdoms.

King Opel II: Indeed, this sword holds immense potential, and it is only fitting that it falls under our jurisdiction. We will ensure its responsible use and protect our realms from any threat.

Rudraksha's eyes narrowed as he listened to their demands. The Chandrahasa sword was a symbol of his kingdom's strength and protection, and he was unwilling to relinquish it to those driven by personal gain.

Rudraksha: King Mizer, King Opel, your demands go against the very essence of our negotiations. This sword is not a mere tool for power, but a sacred artifact that carries a responsibility to safeguard and maintain peace. It cannot be wielded recklessly.

Agastya III: Brother, we must tread carefully. The Chandrahasa sword possesses immense power, and placing it in the wrong hands could have dire consequences.

King Mizer VI: Rudraksha, do not be blinded by your arrogance. We are here to ensure the safety and prosperity of our kingdoms. Hand over the sword, and we will guarantee your protection. Rudraksha's voice hardened as he stood firm in his resolve.

Rudraksha: The Chandrahasa sword belongs to Rudraksham kingdom, and it shall remain so. I will not compromise the security of my people or the balance of the space collective for personal gains.

A heated debate ensued, with tempers flaring and accusations flying across the room. The once-unified summit now found itself at a crossroads, with the possibility of peace slipping away.

King Kratium VI: Enough! This summit was convened to seek a peaceful resolution, not to wage a war over a single artifact. Let us remember the bigger picture and the shared goal of our collective prosperity.

As King Kratium spoke, his words resonated with the other leaders, reminding them of the gravity of their decisions. The atmosphere began to calm, and a realization settled over the council chambers – they needed to rise above their personal desires for the sake of their kingdoms.

"Slowly, King Mizer and King Opel's resolve wavered, as they recognized the importance of unity

and cooperation."

King Mizer VI: Very well, Rudraksha. We shall respect your decision and seek alternative solutions to secure the safety of our kingdoms.

King Opel II: Agreed. Let us not allow our desires to cloud our judgment. The path to peace requires compromise and understanding.

With tensions diffused, the summit regained its momentum, focusing on finding peaceful resolutions, forging alliances, and laying the foundations for a collective defense against external threats.

6

Rope Walk

The atmosphere was charged with anticipation as King Opel II, King Mizer VI, and representatives from Mashrafe Kingdom gathered to discuss their demand for the Chandrahasa sword. King Mizer, bolstered by the presence of the mighty Mashrafe Kingdom, felt emboldened to challenge Rudraksha openly.

The meeting took place in a grand hall, adorned with intricate tapestries and opulent decorations. King Mizer and King Opel sat on one side of a long, polished table, while the delegation from Mashrafe Kingdom occupied the other.

King Mizer VI: Rudraksha, it is time for you to realize the gravity of our demands. We are not to be trifled with. The Chandrahasa sword rightfully belongs to us, and we will stop at nothing to claim it.

King Opel II: Indeed, Rudraksha, your resistance to our demands is futile. The Mashrafes stand with us, and together, we are a force to be reckoned with.

Rudraksha remained calm and composed, his gaze fixed on the representatives from Mashrafe Kingdom. He understood the delicate balance of power in the room and knew that a misstep could tip the scales in favor of aggression.

Rudraksha: King Mizer, King Opel, I recognize your desires, but the Chandrahasa sword is not a pawn to be claimed by force. It serves a greater purpose beyond individual kingdoms' aspirations. It is entrusted to me for the protection and harmony of the entire space collective.

Mashrafe Kingdom's representative, known for their silence and stoicism, finally broke their silence and spoke with measured authority.

Mashrafe Representative: Rudraksha, we understand the significance of the Chandrahasa sword and the responsibilities it carries. While we respect your position as its custodian, we believe that a fair resolution can be reached.

King Mizer VI seized the opportunity to stoke the flames of tension further.

King Mizer VI: Speak up, Mashrafe! You hold the power and influence to sway the outcome. Demand what is rightfully ours!

The Mashrafe representative's eyes narrowed, but they maintained their composed demeanor.

Mashrafe Representative: King Mizer, your impatience is noted. However, we are here to facilitate a peaceful solution, not exacerbate tensions. Let us seek common ground and find a way to address the concerns of all parties involved.

King Opel II couldn't resist provoking Rudraksha further.

King Opel II: Are you truly a king, Rudraksha, or are you just a puppet? A true ruler would recognize the strength of their allies and make the necessary concessions.

Rudraksha's grip on the armrest tightened, his knuckles turning white. He could feel the rising heat of anger within him, but he remained steadfast.

Rudraksha: King Opel, I am no puppet, nor am I blind to the power of our allies. But as a true ruler, I must also consider the greater good and the consequences of handing over the Chandrahasa sword to those driven by selfish desires.

The tension in the room was palpable as Rudraksha and the kings locked eyes, their gazes fierce and unyielding. Amidst the challenge and provocation, the Mashrafe representative's voice cut through the tension like a soothing balm.

Mashrafe Representative: Let us not forget the purpose of our gathering. We must strive for a peaceful resolution that benefits all. The path to unity lies not in aggression, but in understanding and cooperation.

Their words resonated with the leaders, reminding them of their shared goal and the larger picture beyond their individual ambitions. Rudraksha took a deep breath, willing himself to let go of the anger that threatened to consume him. He understood that the journey to peace required patience, diplomacy, and the strength to resist provocation.

Rudraksha: You are right, Mashrafe representative. We must not lose sight of our common objective. Let us continue our dialogue with open minds and seek a solution that ensures harmony and prosperity for all. The room gradually calmed as the leaders redirected their focus toward finding common ground. The delicate balance had been maintained, and the hope for a peaceful resolution flickered like a beacon in the midst of turmoil.

7
Tension showed up

The atmosphere in the room had just started to settle after the heated exchange between Rudraksha, King Mizer, and King Opel. A fragile sense of peace had been restored, with the hope of finding a diplomatic solution. However, the calm was short-lived. King Goister of Goister Kingdom, known for his penchant for stirring trouble, couldn't resist adding fuel to the fire.

King Goister: Is Rudraksha afraid of Mashrafe's might? I sense hesitation in his words. Perhaps he knows that facing the combined force of Mashrafe and its allies will bring him to his knees.

The words hung in the air, causing an immediate shift in the dynamics of the room. The Mashrafe representative's eyes narrowed, a flicker of annoyance passing across their face. Rudraksha's jaw clenched, his gaze fixed on King Goister. He knew that the words were meant to provoke and challenge his resolve.

Rudraksha: King Goister, your words are misplaced. I have never backed down from a fight, nor have I shied away from facing any adversary. My hesitation lies not in fear but in the desire for a peaceful resolution.

The Mashrafe representative remained composed, their eyes searching for a way to diffuse the rising tension.

Mashrafe Representative: Let us not resort to such provocations, King Goister. Our purpose here is to find a peaceful solution, not to incite further hostility. We must respect one another and engage in constructive dialogue.

King Mizer VI, sensing an opportunity to regain control of the situation, joined in the provocation.

King Mizer VI: It seems that Rudraksha's courage falters in the face of our united front. Perhaps he needs a reminder of the consequences he will face if he continues to resist.

King Opel II, his voice laced with a mix of warning and challenge, added his own contribution.

King Opel II: Rudraksha, we have shown great restraint thus far. But do not mistake our patience for weakness. If you do not comply with our demands, the consequences will be severe.

Rudraksha's patience wore thin. His eyes blazed with determination, his voice resonating with unwavering resolve.

Rudraksha: I am not one to be cowed by empty threats, nor will I yield to aggression. I stand for justice, unity, and the protection of the space collective. If you continue to push the limits, know that I will meet your challenge head-on.

The room fell silent as the weight of Rudraksha's words settled upon them. The leaders, once hopeful for a peaceful resolution, found themselves standing at the precipice of conflict once more. Mashrafe, who had been silent throughout the escalating tensions, finally spoke, their voice calm yet firm.

Mashrafe Representative: We implore you all to reconsider your approach. The path of war leads only to destruction and suffering. Let us find a way to unite our strengths for the betterment of all, rather than engaging in senseless confrontation.

Their words carried a subtle plea for reason, a glimmer of hope in the midst of rising hostility.

8
The Voice Of Courage

The room fell into a heavy silence as Rudraksha's heated words echoed through the air. His voice carried a fiery intensity that sent shivers down the spines of everyone present. The force of his words seemed to reverberate, filling the space with an almost tangible energy.

Rudraksha's eyes blazed with a mix of anger and determination. He had reached his breaking point, no longer willing to tolerate the provocations and challenges from King Mizer and King Goister.

Rudraksha: Enough! I will not stand here and listen to your empty threats and baseless accusations any longer. You dare to question my courage, my dedication to our collective well-being? I have fought for justice, protected the weak, and united kingdoms that were once divided. My voice will not be silenced by your attempts to undermine me!

The force of Rudraksha's words was like a thunderclap, silencing the room and freezing everyone in their tracks. Even the bravest among them felt a tremor of uncertainty in the face of his unyielding resolve.

King Mizer and King Goister, who had been so eager to provoke Rudraksha, now found themselves taken aback by the sheer force behind his words. They exchanged glances, their expressions revealing a mixture of surprise and apprehension.

Rudraksha's gaze swept across the room, his voice resolute and commanding.

Rudraksha: I have dedicated myself to the well-being of our space collective, to fostering unity and peace. But make no mistake, I will not hesitate to defend what is rightfully ours. If you choose to challenge me, be prepared to face the consequences. My resolve is unshakable, and I will not falter in the face of adversity.

As Rudraksha's words hung in the air, a profound silence enveloped the room. The tension was palpable, each person processing the weight of his proclamation.
Rudraksha's outburst had shaken the foundations of the room, leaving the leaders contemplating their next move.

The realization dawned upon them that Rudraksha was not a mere figurehead but a force to be reckoned with, one who would fiercely protect his kingdom and the space collective from any threat. The Mashrafe representative, who had remained composed throughout the escalating tension, broke the silence.

Mashrafe Representative: Let us remember why we gathered here today. Our objective is to find a peaceful solution, to unite our strengths for the betterment of all. It is not in our best interest to let our differences lead to unnecessary conflict.

Their words, though softer in tone, carried a weight of reason and diplomacy. Their presence served as a reminder of the potential for cooperation and understanding.

The room slowly began to regain its composure, the lingering echoes of Rudraksha's impassioned words fading into the background. The leaders, humbled by the realization of the consequences of their actions, sought a path forward that would avoid further escalation.

9

Ego matters

The room remained in a fragile state of calm after the words of the Mashrafe representative. Their attempt to diffuse the tension and steer the conversation towards a peaceful resolution had momentarily brought a glimmer of hope.

However, Rudraksha, unwilling to let the accusations against Mashrafe go unanswered, broke the silence once again. His voice carried a mix of determination and accusation.

Rudraksha: I am well aware of the intentions that lie beneath your words, Mashrafe. You claim to seek peace and understanding, but your true desire is the possession of the Chandrahasa sword. Do not attempt to deny it any longer.

The Mashrafe representative remained composed, meeting Rudraksha's gaze with an unwavering stare. Their silence spoke volumes, neither confirming nor denying the accusation. King Mizer, seeing an opportunity to gain the favor of Mashrafe, saw fit to interject with a daring voice.

King Mizer: Rudraksha, if Mashrafe's desire for the Chandrahasa sword is what it takes to secure their support, then so be it. Perhaps it is time you considered involving Mashrafe in our affairs. Otherwise, they may forget about this pursuit of peace altogether.

The audacity of King Mizer's statement hung in the air, challenging Rudraksha openly. The room held its breath, waiting for Rudraksha's response.

Rudraksha's eyes narrowed, a flicker of anger crossing his face. The weight of the situation bore down upon him, but he remained resolute.

Rudraksha: I will not succumb to such pressure, nor will I compromise the principles that have guided me thus far. The Chandrahasa sword is a symbol of justice and protection, not a bargaining chip to be exploited. I will not allow it to fall into the wrong hands.

His words echoed with determination, drawing a line in the sand. The challenge had been issued, and Rudraksha stood firmly on the side of righteousness.

Mashrafe, still composed, observed the exchange with a calculating gaze. Their intentions remained enigmatic, their true loyalties hidden beneath a veil of diplomacy.

The room buzzed with tension, the leaders realizing that they were at a crossroads. The path to peace seemed uncertain, overshadowed by conflicting desires and egos.

10

Storm King Goister's laughter pierced the tension in the room, his words dripping with mockery. King Goister: Rudraksha, it seems that all you can do

King Goister's laughter pierced the tension in the room, his words dripping with mockery.

King Goister: Rudraksha, it seems that all you can do is boast about your power. But deep down, you fear Mashrafe's might. Admit it, Rudraksha, you are no match for us.

Rudraksha's eyes blazed with a mix of fury and resolve. He felt the weight of Goister's words, the challenge to his authority and strength. However, he refused to let it break his composure.

Rudraksha: Fear does not drive me, Goister. It is the responsibility to protect my kingdom and its people that fuels my actions. I seek peace and harmony, not the chaos of war. But make no mistake, if pushed, I will defend what is mine with all my might.

King Mashrafe, who had remained silent until now, finally spoke, his voice laced with caution.

King Mashrafe: Rudraksha, I understand the danger we all face. It is not a matter to be taken lightly. However, the Chandrahasa sword holds immense power, and its possession must be approached with great care. We cannot ignore the potential consequences that come with it.

King Opel, interrupted the gathering with a commanding presence.

King Opel: Enough! Rudraksha is not one to cower in fear. He seeks peace, not dominance. We must not let suspicious and doubt cloud our judgment. Instead, we should focus on finding a way to ensure the safety of all kingdoms involved.

His words carried authority, a reminder of the delicate balance that needed to be maintained. Yet, the underlying tension in the room remained palpable.

King Opel: We cannot let Rudraksha dictate the terms. If he refuses to acknowledge the potential alliance between Mashrafe and our kingdoms, then we must show him the strength we possess. We shall not be silenced or overlooked.

The room became a battleground of conflicting voices, each kingdom vying for its interests and beliefs. The once-promising path to peace was now obscured by rising animosity and mistrust.

Rudraksha's gaze swept across the room, his resolve firm and unyielding. He knew that the road ahead would be fraught with challenges, but he remained steadfast in his pursuit of a peaceful solution. The situation had reached a tipping point, and the impending storm of conflict loomed ever closer.

11

Fracture of the Truce

As the tension in the room escalated, Geame, the powerful prince of the Marcowich Kingdom and a neutral observer, broke the silence with a measured tone.

Geame: It is becoming increasingly evident that King Opel, along with his allies, is the one provoking Rudraksha. The atmosphere is thick with hostility, and it is hindering any meaningful progress towards a resolution.

King Kratium, recognizing the need for a pause in the proceedings, intervened.

King Kratium: Perhaps it would be wise to postpone this meeting until tomorrow. Emotions are running high, and a moment of respite might help us approach the situation with clearer minds.

Rudraksha, who had remained composed throughout the heated exchanges, spoke up with determination.

Rudraksha: While I understand the importance of discussing matters thoroughly, Rudraksham Kingdom is not a small entity like Opel. I cannot afford to be here for days on end, wasting precious time while my kingdom's fate hangs in the balance.

The room fell into a hushed silence, the weight of Rudraksha's words lingering in the air. The other kings exchanged glances, realizing the significance of the situation. It was clear that Rudraksha's patience was wearing thin, and further delays could lead to dire consequences.

King Opel, sensing the urgency in Rudraksha's tone, spoke cautiously, trying to salvage the fragile truce.

King Opel: I understand your concerns, Rudraksha. We must find a way to expedite the resolution without compromising its integrity. Let us reconvene tomorrow, prepared to engage in fruitful discussions and seek a peaceful way forward.

The room, though filled with lingering tension, begrudgingly accepted the suggestion. The meeting was adjourned, giving each kingdom time to reflect on their stance and consider the consequences of their actions.

Rudraksha, accompanied by Agastya, left the court with a firm resolve. The realization that the delicate peace they had hoped for was slipping away fueled their determination to find a swift and decisive resolution.

The stage was set for a critical juncture in the proceedings, where every word and action would shape the fate of the kingdoms involved. The path to peace remained uncertain, and the weight of responsibility lay heavy on Rudraksha's shoulders. As the sun set on that eventful day, the seeds of discord had been sown, and the impending choices would test the strength of alliances and the true intentions of those involved.

12

Nightmare

After the meeting was called off, each king was assigned a palace to stay for the duration of their negotiations. Time passed, and the tension in the air lingered like a heavy fog. Among the kings, Mashrafe felt an increasing unease, as he earnestly desired to avoid a confrontation with Rudraksha.

Marfel, on the other hand, deliberated with his trusted courtiers, seeking possible avenues to establish a friendship with Rudraksha and avert further conflict.

As the night settled upon the kingdoms, casting a blanket of darkness across the sky, King Opel and King Goister, ever the instigators, caught sight of Rudraksha standing alone, gazing up at the majestic star-filled expanse. Their egos flared, and they saw an opportunity to provoke their rival.

King Opel, accompanied by Goister, approached Rudraksha, striding with an air of arrogance. They maneuvered their spaceship to hover menacingly in front of Rudraksha, flexing their technological prowess.

Opel: (smirking) Ah, Rudraksha, do you see the might of our kingdom? Our technological advancements far surpass anything your Rudraksham Kingdom can muster.

Goister: (chuckling) Indeed, Rudraksha, your outdated ways and primitive weapons pale in comparison to our formidable arsenal. We are the future, while you are stuck in the past.

Rudraksha remained steadfast, his eyes fixed on the spectacle before him. He had long anticipated such taunts and displays of power, but his unwavering spirit was unshaken.

Rudraksha: (calmly) Opel, Goister, your ostentatious displays do not intimidate me. True strength lies not in the size of your ships or the reach of your weapons but in the valor and integrity of one's heart. It is a lesson you both seem to have forgotten.

Opel's smirk faded, replaced by a scowl of frustration. Goister's laughter turned into a sneer. Their attempts at provocation were met with resilience, and it unsettled them.

Opel: (through gritted teeth) You may think yourself superior, Rudraksha, but we shall prove your arrogance wrong. The Chandrahasa sword will be ours, and your kingdom will bow before us.

Goister: (menacingly) Indeed, Rudraksha, your defiance will be your downfall. Prepare yourself for the reckoning that awaits you.

With that, Opel and Goister retreated, leaving Rudraksha alone with his thoughts under the starlit sky. The encounter had only reinforced his resolve and deepened his determination to safeguard his kingdom's honor and secure a peaceful resolution.

Meanwhile, Marfel, who had witnessed the confrontation from a distance, took note of Opel and Goister's behavior. He understood the gravity of the situation and the need for diplomacy. With newfound clarity, Marfel resolved to find a way to bridge the divide between Rudraksham Kingdom and his own.

The night carried on, and the kingdoms braced themselves for the challenges that lay ahead. The stage was set for intricate maneuvers and strategic alliances, as the fate of the realms hung precariously in the balance.

13

The Arrival of Suryahasa

After the encounter with King Opel and King Goister, Rudraksha knew he needed to take decisive action. He reached out to Suryahasa, a trusted ally renowned for his mastery of advanced technology. Rudraksha requested the presence of his personal royal aircraft, a vessel that emitted powerful waves capable of disrupting radars and disabling space protection weapons.

As the appointed time arrived, Rudraksha's aircraft soared through the vast expanse of space, swiftly approaching the boundaries of the area where the kings were staying. The skies crackled with energy as the powerful waves emitted by the aircraft disrupted the delicate systems of surveillance and defense.

Within moments, radars malfunctioned, sending warning signals into chaos. Space protection weapons malfunctioned, their beams dissipating into harmless sparks. The arrival of Rudraksha's aircraft was both a testament to his power and a declaration of his determination.

The other kings, Marfel, Mizer, and Opel, watched in awe and trepidation as Rudraksha's vessel descended, gracefully landing on the ground with a resounding thud. The surrounding area trembled slightly under its immense weight.

Rudraksha emerged from his aircraft, radiating an aura of authority and strength. His eyes gleamed with unwavering resolve as he surveyed the stunned onlookers. The tension in the air was palpable as everyone waited for Rudraksha's next move.

Rudraksha: (in a commanding voice) Kings of the Mashrafe, Marcowich, and Opel Kingdoms, I have summoned you here to resolve the escalating tensions and bring an end to this senseless conflict. It is time we put aside our differences and work towards a peaceful resolution.

His words echoed with conviction, and for a moment, the gravity of the situation settled upon the hearts of the gathered monarchs. Marfel, Mashrafe, Mizer, and Opel exchanged glances, silently acknowledging the power and determination displayed before them.

Marfel: (with a measured tone) Rudraksha, we understand the consequences of further escalation. We are willing to engage in meaningful dialogue to find a peaceful solution. Let us set aside our differences and seek common ground for the benefit of all our kingdoms.

Mashrafe: (nodding) I concur. The path of diplomacy is far more preferable than that of war. Let us find a way to resolve our grievances and ensure a harmonious coexistence.

Mizer and Opel, though initially taken aback by Rudraksha's grand entrance, realized the significance of the moment. The powerful waves emitted by his aircraft served as a stark reminder of the might Rudraksham Kingdom possessed.

Mizer: (grudgingly) Very well, Rudraksha. We shall heed your call for peace, for now. But do not mistake this for weakness. We shall not forget the strength of our kingdoms.

Opel: (through clenched teeth) Agreed, Rudraksha. Let us engage in constructive dialogue and seek a resolution that ensures the preservation of our respective realms.

With the tension momentarily diffused, Rudraksha's eyes softened, revealing a glimmer of hope for a peaceful future. The stage was set for a crucial discussion, where the fate of the kingdoms would be determined not by the clash of weapons but by the power of diplomacy and understanding.

14

Felicity

As the atmosphere still crackled with the remnants of Rudraksha's powerful waves, Geame, the Prince of Marcowich Kingdom, observed the scene before him. While the other kings and their kingdoms were in awe of Rudraksha's aircraft, a spark of competitiveness ignited within Geame.

Determined to assert the strength of his kingdom, Geame reached out to his trusted general and requested the presence of his sister, Felicity, the revered Goddess of Spirits. Felicity possessed an aircraft renowned for its sheer power and awe-inspiring capabilities.

The skies above the gathering darkened, signaling the arrival of Felicity's aircraft. As it descended, a dazzling display of radiance accompanied its every movement. The sheer magnitude of its presence caused weaker structures to crumble under the intensity of the rays it carried.

The onlookers, including Rudraksha, Marfel, Mashrafe, Mizer, and Opel, watched with a mix of astonishment and trepidation as Felicity's aircraft settled on the ground. The air seemed to vibrate with the sheer power that emanated from its magnificent form.

Geame stepped forward, his chest puffed with pride, and a glint of mischief danced in his eyes. He knew that the arrival of Felicity's aircraft would leave an indelible impression on the assembled monarchs.

Geame: (with an air of confidence) Rudraksha, I present to you the might of Marcowich Kingdom, embodied by my sister, Felicity, and her awe-inspiring aircraft. Let this serve as a reminder that Marcowich Kingdom stands as a force to be reckoned with.

Rudraksha maintained his composure, observing the grand display before him. He recognized the inherent need within each kingdom to assert their power and prove their worth. However, he remained resolute in his commitment to pursue a peaceful resolution.

Rudraksha: (calmly) Geame, your kingdom's power is indeed formidable, as is evident from the arrival of Felicity's aircraft. But let us remember that our goal here is to find a peaceful solution, to forge alliances rather than fuel further animosity. May we seek understanding and common ground in this pivotal moment.

Felicity, radiating an air of mystique and grace, stepped out of her aircraft. The aura of the Goddess of Spirits filled the space, momentarily captivating the attention of those present. She glanced at Rudraksha with a mix of curiosity and respect, recognizing the strength and determination he possessed.

Felicity: (with a soft voice) Rudraksha, I have witnessed the power and majesty of your kingdom. Let us channel our strengths not towards conflict, but towards building bridges of harmony and mutual respect. Together, we can achieve greatness.

Marfel, Mizer, and Opel, who had been observing the exchange, felt a renewed sense of hope. The arrival of

Felicity's aircraft, while initially triggering a sense of rivalry, also symbolized the potential for unity and collaboration among the kingdoms.

Marfel: (smiling) Indeed, Felicity. Let us set aside our differences and embrace the spirit of cooperation. The time for understanding and diplomacy has come.

Marfel: I concur. The display of power should serve as a reminder of our collective strength, which can be harnessed for the greater good.

Mizer and Opel exchanged glances, realizing the importance of unity in the face of their shared goals. The overwhelming presence of Rudraksha and Felicity's aircraft left an indelible impression on them, highlighting the need to find common ground.

Mizer: (reluctantly) Rudraksha, Felicity, let us put aside our differences and work towards a peaceful resolution. Our kingdoms hold immense power, and together, we can shape the future.

Opel: (firmly) Agreed. We shall engage in open dialogue and seek a solution that benefits all, leaving behind the animosity that has clouded our judgments.

With the stage now set for a new phase of discussions, the kingdoms of Rudraksham, Mashrafe, Marcowich, and Opel stood on the precipice of a transformative journey. The might of their aircraft had not only showcased their power but also presented an opportunity for unity and understanding.

15

First Bump

As the tension continued to mount, Marfel, the ruler of Mashrafe Kingdom, contemplated the unfolding events. With both Rudraksham and Marcowich Kingdoms showcasing their impressive aircraft, Marfel realized the need to assert the might and prowess of Mashrafe Kingdom. It was time for Mashrafe to make its mark.

Marfel swiftly contacted his kingdom and requested the deployment of their most guarded secret—the special aircraft known as "Furst." Constructed with the strongest material in the universe, Furst was a testament to Mashrafe's technological advancements and unwavering determination.

The skies shimmered with anticipation as Furst made its way towards the gathering. Its sleek design and unparalleled capabilities were the talk of legends. As it approached the horizon, a wave of awe washed over the onlookers, momentarily halting their discussions.

Rudraksha, Felicity, Mizer, Opel, and Geame watched with a mix of curiosity and apprehension as Furst descended. The ground beneath them seemed to tremble ever so slightly, echoing the impending clash of powers.

Marfel stepped forward, radiating confidence and resolve. He knew that this moment would forever shape the course of their interactions. With each stride, he showcased the authority and might of Mashrafe Kingdom.

Marfel: (in a commanding voice) Rudraksha, Felicity, esteemed kings and queens, behold the strength of Mashrafe Kingdom—the embodiment of resilience and ingenuity. Furst stands as a symbol of our unwavering commitment to protect our people and preserve peace. Let us find a way to unite our strengths rather than engaging in a futile display of power.

Rudraksha's gaze met Marfel's, recognizing the unwavering determination in the eyes of the Mashrafe ruler. A flicker of respect and understanding passed between them, signaling a glimmer of hope in the midst of growing tension.

Felicity: (with a calm voice) Marfel, your kingdom's might is truly remarkable. The presence of Furst speaks volumes about your dedication to peace and prosperity. Let us channel our energies towards finding a resolution that benefits us all.

Mizer, Opel, and Geame, who had been observing the unfolding events, felt a renewed sense of urgency. The combined power and determination of Rudraksham, Marchowich, and Mashrafe Kingdoms left no room for doubt—they were forces to be reckoned with.

Mizer: (grudgingly) Marfel, you have made a bold statement with the arrival of Furst. Let us set aside our differences and focus on the task at hand. Our kingdoms possess immense potential, and together, we can achieve remarkable feats.

Opel: (nodding) Agreed. The time for posturing and provocation has passed. We must embrace the opportunity for cooperation and understanding.

Geame, observing the shifting dynamics, realized the futility of further escalation. He, too, understood the significance of unity and collaboration in the face of greater challenges.

Geame: (with a determined voice) It is time for us to stand together, for the greater good of our realms. Let us set aside our egos and work towards a peaceful solution.

The assembled monarchs and their representatives acknowledged the gravity of the situation. The arrival of Furst had undeniably heightened the stakes, leaving no room for frivolous banter or unnecessary aggression. The time for decisive action had arrived.

However, as the kingdoms paused to consider their next moves, a foreboding sense of uncertainty lingered in the air. The clash of mighty aircraft had intensified the competitive spirit, and the path to resolution remained elusive.

16

Seeds

———♡———

In the confines of their private chambers, King Mizer, King Goister, and King Opel convened for a clandestine meeting. The weight of their realization hung heavy in the air—their kingdoms stood no chance against the combined might of Rudraksham, Mashrafe, and Marchowich Kingdoms.

King Goister, known for his cunning strategies, contemplated a new plan—one that aimed to sow discord within the united front of their opponents. He knew that dividing their forces would weaken their overall strength, potentially tipping the balance in their favor.

King Goister: (leaning in, his voice dripping with mischief) Gentlemen, it's clear to us that a direct confrontation against Rudraksham, Mashrafe, and Marchowich Kingdoms would be futile. Our only hope lies in finding a way to exploit the cracks within their alliance.

King Mizer: (stroking his beard, deep in thought) How do you propose we achieve that, Goister? Rudraksha, Marfel, and Geame have formed a strong bond, and their kingdoms appear united in their cause.

King Opel: (smirking) We must create a situation that stirs distrust and fuels their internal conflicts. If we succeed in pitting them against each other, their unity will crumble, and our chances of victory will increase.

King Goister: (nodding) Precisely, Opel. We need to find a way to exploit their vulnerabilities. We know that Rudraksha is known for his hot-headed nature. If we can manipulate his emotions, he might act impulsively, causing a rift between Rudraksham and the other kingdoms.

King Mizer: (intrigued) And what about Marchowich and Mashrafe? How do we incite discord among them?

King Goister: (with a devious smile) We exploit their differences, their conflicting ambitions. Mashrafe seeks power and control, while Marchowich values harmony and peace. If we can manipulate their desires and plant seeds of doubt, we can create fissures within their alliance.

King Opel: (leaning forward) It won't be easy, but with careful planning and strategic moves, we can weaken their bond and turn their strengths against each other. The path to victory lies in their division.

As their sinister plot began to take shape, the three kings exchanged knowing glances. The road ahead would be treacherous, but they were willing to push the boundaries of morality to secure their own kingdoms' survival.

Little did they know that the winds of discord they sought to harness could unleash unforeseen consequences, threatening not only their opponents but their own realms as well.

In the shadows, their plan began to unfold—a calculated dance of manipulation, whispers of deceit, and subtle actions that would set the stage for the chaos they hoped to create.

17
Unity Cracker

As the night grew deeper, Rudraksha lay awake in his chamber, contemplating the words that had ignited a spark within him. King Goister's audacity and cunning had left a deep impression on him, and the more Rudraksha thought about it, the more he realized the potential consequences of an alliance between Marchowich and Mashrafe kingdoms.

Rudraksha's mind wandered, considering the delicate balance of power and the history of rivalry between the two kingdoms. Marchowich, with its thirst for dominion, and Mashrafe, with its quest for harmony, had always been at odds. And now, with the unity of the three powerful kingdoms at stake, the dormant animosity threatened to resurface.

Rudraksha knew that he couldn't dismiss King Goister's words entirely. While their intent was undoubtedly manipulative, there was an underlying truth—the alliance forged among Rudraksham, Mashrafe, and Marchowich Kingdoms was tenuous at best. Each kingdom had its own agenda, its own aspirations for greatness.

In the early hours of the morning, Rudraksha rose from his bed, his mind set on uncovering the truth. He summoned his trusted advisers and commanders to a secret meeting.

Rudraksha: (with determination) My loyal companions, we stand at a critical juncture. King Goister's words echo in my mind, and I cannot ignore the potential danger they represent. We must delve deeper into the relationship between Marchowich and Mashrafe.

General Arkan: (furrowing his brow) My king, we have always been wary of Marchowich's thirst for power. It wouldn't be surprising if they sought to exploit the unity we have established with Mashrafe.

Rudraksha: (nodding) Exactly, Arkan. We need to assess the extent of their allegiance. I want you to gather every piece of intelligence available to us regarding any secret negotiations or communications between Marchowich and Mashrafe.

The command was issued, and the wheels were set in motion. Spies were dispatched, their ears to the ground, gathering information that would unveil the true nature of the relationship between the rival kingdoms.

Meanwhile, tensions simmered within Marchowich and Mashrafe as well. Geame, the prince of Marchowich, had witnessed the powerful display of Rudraksha's might and feared the unity of the three kingdoms. He too questioned the intentions of Mashrafe, sensing a hidden agenda behind their professed desire for peace.

Prince Geame: (addressing his council) Brothers and sisters,our alliance with Mashrafe raises concerns. Their pursuit of harmony seems too idealistic, and we cannot afford to let our guard down.

Council Member Felicity: (narrowing her eyes) Geame, I sense a hidden motive behind their professed desire for peace. We must tread carefully and evaluate their actions.

As Geame and his council pondered the situation, news arrived that Marchowich spies had intercepted rumors of secret communications between Mashrafe and a third party. Whispers of doubt and suspicion filled the air, threatening to unravel the fragile threads that held the three kingdoms together.

The stage was set for a confrontation—a battle of wits, power, and loyalties. The alliances forged in the face of a common enemy now faced the ultimate test of trust.

Unknown to all, the seeds of discord sown by King Goister were beginning to sprout. The careful balance of power and unity that had been established hung by a thread, and the once-unbreakable alliance now teetered on the precipice of chaos.

In the shadows, the puppeteers reveled in their machinations, knowing that their actions were about to set in motion a chain of events that would reshape the destiny of the space collective of all universes.

18
Calculate and Gamble

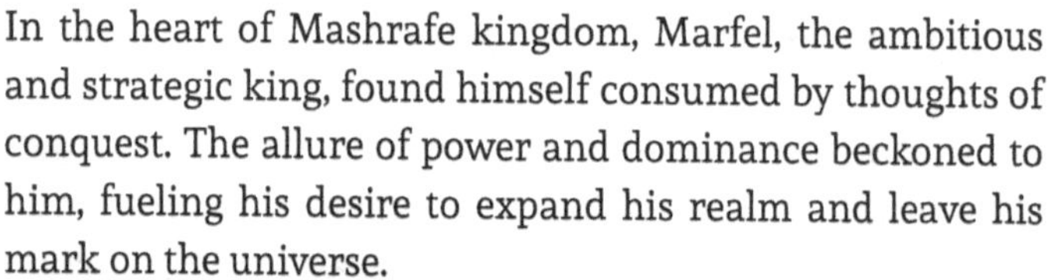

In the heart of Mashrafe kingdom, Marfel, the ambitious and strategic king, found himself consumed by thoughts of conquest. The allure of power and dominance beckoned to him, fueling his desire to expand his realm and leave his mark on the universe.

Marfel: (whispering to himself) Marchowich kingdom... they have always been our rivals. Their lust for power and territory knows no bounds. If we could seize their lands, their resources, we would solidify our position as the supreme force in this realm.

His mind ablaze with possibilities, Marfel summoned his trusted advisers and military strategists to discuss his audacious plan.

Marfel: (leaning forward) My esteemed council, the time for peace and unity may be coming to an end. The foundations of trust among our kingdoms have grown fragile, and I believe Marchowich holds a hidden advantage over us. We cannot afford to be caught unaware.

General Kael: (raising an eyebrow) Your Majesty, are you suggesting we wage war against Marchowich kingdom?

Marfel: (smirking) War, my dear General, may be an inevitability. But we shall approach it with cunning and precision. I have devised a plan—one that capitalizes on the strength of our forces and exploits a weakness within Marchowich.

The council leaned in, their curiosity piqued by Marfel's words. He unfolded his strategy, outlining a plan to exploit the power of Felicity, Geame's elder sister and the goddess of spirits.

Marfel: (contemplating) Felicity possesses a power that surpasses the might of the Chandrahasa sword—an army of spirits at her command. If we can sway her allegiance, we will possess an unstoppable force.

The council members exchanged glances, considering the audacity of the plan. They knew that the manipulation of a goddess came with great risks and consequences.

Advisor Leandra: (cautioning) Your Majesty, approaching a goddess is no small matter. We must tread carefully and consider the repercussions of such a course of action.

Marfel: (nodding) You are wise, Leandra. We shall proceed cautiously. Felicity holds the key to Marchowich's power, and by gaining her support, we undermine their foundation.

Meanwhile, in the corridors of Marchowich kingdom, Geame grappled with his own doubts and suspicions. He had heard whispers of Marfel's ambitions, of his desires to conquer their realm. The fragility of their unity, once a source of strength, now threatened to crumble under the weight of doubt.

Geame: (muttering to himself) Marfel's hunger for power knows no bounds. But we cannot let our guard down. We must protect our kingdom and ensure its sovereignty.

Felicity, the goddess of spirits, sensed the growing tension and unease within her brother and the kingdom. She knew that her powers held the potential to sway the course of events. Yet, she also understood the delicate balance of power and the consequences of her choices.

Felicity: (whispering to the spirits) My loyal companions, we find ourselves at a crossroads. The fate of Marchowich hangs in the balance. We must choose our path wisely.

As Marfel's plan took shape and Geame sought to protect his kingdom, the stage was set for a clash of ambitions, where the allure of power and the desire to control would test the limits of alliances.

In the shadows, unseen forces stirred, ready to exploit the discord and exploit any opportunity that presented itself.

19

Power Equation

The balance of power in the realm hung delicately, as Rudraksham Kingdom, Marchowich Kingdom, and Mashrafe Kingdom stood as the paramount forces, each harboring its own arsenal of strength and ambition.

Rudraksha, with his unrivaled powers and command over the legendary Chandrahasa sword, was revered as one of the most formidable beings in the collective. His indomitable spirit and prowess were matched only by his strategic acumen.

Meanwhile, Geame, the prince of Marchowich Kingdom, possessed his own remarkable abilities, augmented further by the presence of his sister, Felicity—the goddess of spirits. Their combined might and connection to ethereal forces made them a formidable duo in their own right.

Yet, beneath the surface of their power, a subtle undercurrent threatened to disrupt the balance. Agastya, Rudraksha's enigmatic brother and master of dark energy, loomed as a potential game-changer. His abilities were shrouded in mystery, and whispers of his dark intentions pervaded the realm.

Rudraksha: (contemplating) Agastya, my brother... a force to be reckoned with. His mastery of dark energy poses a grave threat not only to Marchowich Kingdom but to our very existence. We must not underestimate his power.

Geame: (with conviction) Indeed, Rudraksha. Agastya's malevolence is matched only by his prowess. Felicity, as the goddess of spirits, holds great strength, but even she is vulnerable to the darkness he wields. We must remain vigilant.

As the three kingdoms braced for the impending clash, the looming question of supremacy weighed heavily on their minds. The uncertainty of the outcome fueled a desire to secure alliances and forge new paths.

Rudraksha, aware of the delicate balance, sought to solidify his position and strengthen his alliances. He called upon his trusted advisers to devise a strategy that would tip the scales in their favor.

Advisor Surya: (suggesting) Your Majesty, while Marchowich Kingdom possesses great power, it would be wise to seek additional allies. Our cause could be strengthened through strategic alliances with neighboring realms.

Rudraksha: (nodding) You speak truth, Surya. We must expand our web of alliances to ensure our supremacy. We cannot afford to face the combined forces of Marchowich and Mashrafe kingdoms alone.

Meanwhile, Geame, burdened by the knowledge of Agastya's threat, convened a council to discuss the next course of action. They contemplated ways to fortify their defenses and uncover Agastya's weaknesses.

General Alaric: (pondering) Your Highness, Agastya's dark energy is formidable, but not insurmountable. We must delve deeper into the ancient texts, seeking knowledge of his vulnerabilities. There may lie our key to victory.

Geame: (determined) Agastya must be confronted and neutralized. Our alliance with Rudraksham Kingdom can aid us in this endeavor. Together, we shall overcome the darkness that looms over our realms.

As the leaders strategized and sought to leverage their strengths, the fate of the realm hung in the balance. The clash between Rudraksham, Marchowich, and Mashrafe kingdoms drew nearer, and the stakes grew higher with every passing moment.

Unknown to them all, unseen forces moved in the shadows, orchestrating their own agendas and aiming to exploit the fractures that threatened the fragile unity of the kingdoms.

In the face of mounting tensions and the ever-present threat of Agastya, the resolve of each kingdom would be tested, their alliances forged.

20

Ego wins

The court for the peace settlement convened once again, but this time, the dynamics had shifted. Rudraksha, Geame, and Marfel—representing Rudraksham, Marchowich, and Mashrafe kingdoms respectively—found themselves consumed by their ego and the preservation of their prestige.

Rudraksha, standing tall with the Chandrahasa sword by his side, exuded an air of invincibility. His eyes burned with determination, unwilling to yield an inch of his power and dominion. The memories of previous provocations and challenges lingered, fueling a desire to assert his authority.

Geame, his gaze fierce and resolute, carried the weight of Marchowich Kingdom's legacy. The echoes of his ancestors' triumphs and defeats resounded within him, pushing him to safeguard their honor and sovereignty.

Marfel, the stoic king of Mashrafe Kingdom, wore a mask of calm determination. Though he sought to avoid conflict and valued peace, the mounting tensions and the ever-present threat of Agastya had kindled a fire within him. His allegiance to his people and the security of his kingdom spurred him to stand his ground.

The atmosphere in the court crackled with an electrifying tension as the three rulers met eye to eye. The air was heavy with unspoken words, each one silently challenging the others to back down.

Rudraksha: (in a low, firm voice) Peace may have been a consideration once, but the provocations and insults endured cannot be forgotten. The time for compromise is over. We shall defend our sovereignty and power with unwavering resolve.

Geame: (with a steely gaze) Marchowich Kingdom has withstood countless trials throughout history. We will not cower or bow to any kingdom's whims. Our legacy demands us to face challenges head-on, for it is through strength that we prevail.

Marfel: (calmly but firmly) I, too, value peace and harmony, but I will not let my kingdom be threatened or undermined. Mashrafe Kingdom shall stand its ground, prepared to defend its people and honor.

As the rulers made their impassioned declarations, tension hung in the air, threatening to ignite a spark that could engulf the realms in a devastating conflict. The fragile threads of peace appeared to unravel, overshadowed by the inflamed egos and the unyielding pride of the three kingdoms.

The courtiers, advisers, and onlookers watched with bated breath, their eyes darting between the powerful rulers, their fates hanging in the balance.

Surya: (whispering to Rudraksha) Your Majesty, the path of peace may seem arduous, but there are lives at stake. Consider the consequences of a war that engulfs our realms. We must find a way to negotiate and preserve what we hold dear.

Geame's General Alaric, ever loyal and committed to the cause, approached him with a similar sentiment.

General Alaric: (urging Geame) Your Highness, the strength of Marchowich Kingdom lies not only in our might but also in our ability to exercise restraint and wisdom. Let us explore avenues of diplomacy and mutual understanding.

Marfel, surrounded by his trusted council, contemplated the weight of his decision. The responsibility of safeguarding his kingdom's prosperity weighed heavily upon him.

Marfel: (addressing his council) The path we tread is treacherous, but the preservation of life and harmony should be our ultimate goal. Let us exhaust all avenues of diplomacy and find a way to ease these tensions without sacrificing our dignity.

As the rulers and their advisers grappled with their decisions, the court remained shrouded in an uneasy stillness. The fate of the realms teetered on a knife's edge, the echoes of pride and ego threatening to tip the delicate balance towards conflict.

In the next chapter, the rulers would face their greatest test yet—the challenge of reconciling their desires for power and prestige with the responsibility to protect their people and forge a path towards peace.

21

The manipulations

King Goister, seizing the opportune moment, saw the growing tensions between Marchowich and Rudraksham kingdoms as an ideal situation to spark the war he desired. Collaborating with King Mizer, they delved into strategizing ways to incite conflict between the two powerful realms.

After careful deliberation, they identified a potential weak link in the form of Hemsmen, the spouse of Felicity and ruler of Marchowich Kingdom. They knew Hemsmen to be easily swayed and manipulated, and they saw an opportunity to exploit his vulnerabilities.

King Mizer, taking charge of the plan, crafted a cunning message filled with veiled provocations. The message was designed to play on Hemsmen's insecurities and goad him into taking a reckless course of action.

Hemsmen, unaware of the intricate machinations taking place behind the scenes, received the message. Blinded by a surge of misplaced pride and a desire to assert his authority, he succumbed to the manipulations and hastily made a grave decision.

Without consulting Rudraksha or considering the delicate situation at hand, Hemsmen sent a warning message to the Rudraksham Kingdom. The message carried a threatening undertone, a show of defiance and misplaced confidence.

Within the walls of Rudraksham Kingdom, the royal family members who were overseeing the empire in Rudraksha's absence received the message. They were taken aback by the audacity of Hemsmen's actions, their hearts heavy with disappointment and concern.

Amidst the peace settlement discussions, the revelation of Hemsmen's rash decision sent shockwaves through the realm. It was a betrayal of trust and a perilous step towards the brink of war.

Rudraksha, alerted to the situation, felt a surge of frustration and disappointment. He had sought peace and understanding, but his efforts seemed to be unraveling at the seams. The delicate threads that held the realms together were being tested, and the consequences of this misstep weighed heavily upon him.

In the next chapter, the ripple effects of Hemsmen's ill-fated decision would ripple through the corridors of power, further escalating tensions and raising the stakes for all involved.

22

Suryahasa: The monster

Rudraksha seethed with anger upon learning of Hemsmen's ill-conceived message. His mind raced with thoughts of retribution and swift action, intending to annihilate Hemsmen's bloodline for his audacity. He began preparing himself to journey to Marchowich Kingdom and unleash his wrath upon the misguided ruler.

Amidst this tempest of fury, Suryahasa, the grandson of Chandrahasa, approached Rudraksha. With a calm demeanor, he sought to temper the storm that brewed within Rudraksha's heart. Suryahasa understood the weight of Rudraksha's power and the responsibilities that came with it.

Speaking with a voice imbued with wisdom, Suryahasa addressed Rudraksha, "**Oh, Supreme Rudraksha**, your might and influence are known throughout the realms. But engaging in direct conflict with a ruler of such insignificance would only demean your exalted position. Allow me, your loyal companion and descendant of Chandrahasa, to confront Hemsmen on your behalf."

Rudraksha, though still enveloped in anger, paused to listen to Suryahasa's words. The sheer reverence and respect in Suryahasa's voice held sway over his emotions. He realized the truth in Suryahasa's words – engaging in a direct confrontation would be beneath his stature.

With a solemn nod, Rudraksha acquiesced, recognizing the wisdom in Suryahasa's counsel. "Suryahasa, my loyal companion and bearer of the bloodline, I trust in your strength and understanding. Bring an end to this waywardness and restore the balance that has been disrupted," Rudraksha responded, his voice laced with determination.

Suryahasa's face bore a mixture of determination and loyalty as he accepted the task entrusted to him. "I shall carry forth the might of Chandrahasa and the essence of our bloodline. Hemsmen shall face the consequences of his actions," Suryahasa vowed, his words resonating with a sense of purpose.

The discussion between Rudraksha and Suryahasa came to a close, their shared understanding casting a sense of reassurance. The weight of the impending confrontation was now shifted onto Suryahasa's shoulders, as he prepared to embark on a journey that would shape the fate of the kingdoms.

As the chapter drew to a close, Rudraksha's anger simmered, replaced by a glimmer of hope that Suryahasa's intervention would restore the delicate balance and avert further calamity. Only time would reveal the consequences of their decisions and the impact they would have on the destiny of the realms.

23
Suryahasa's Fury

Hemsmen, ignorant of the impending doom that awaited him, reveled in his delusion of power. He boasted proudly of the warning he had sent to Rudraksha, unaware of the storm that was about to descend upon him. Little did he know that the wrath of Suryahasa, backed by the might of Rudraksham Kingdom, was poised to unleash its fury.

As Suryahasa and the fleet of Rudraksham aircraft pierced through the borders of Hemsmen's domain, chaos ensued. Panic gripped the hearts of the unsuspecting military general and his forces. The sheer presence of Suryahasa and his army sent shockwaves through the ranks, as the realization of their impending doom set in.

Fuelled by a burning rage, Suryahasa spared no moment for diplomatic talks or negotiations. With a swift and merciless onslaught, he and the formidable forces of Rudraksham Kingdom embarked on a ruthless campaign, cutting down anyone who dared to stand in their path. The air resonated with the screams of Hemsmen's subjects and the clash of steel against steel.

Within a mere hour, the once-proud Hemsmen lay defeated and broken at Suryahasa's feet. His delusions of grandeur shattered, replaced by the harsh reality of his folly. Suryahasa's fury had swept through Hemsmen's domain like a tempest, leaving nothing but devastation in its wake.

The chapter came to an abrupt end, leaving behind a trail of destruction and foreshadowing the continuation of the war that loomed on the horizon. In the subsequent chapter, the consequences of Suryahasa's wrath and the ramifications of Hemsmen's defeat would unfold, setting the stage for further conflict and a battle that would shake the foundations of the realms.

24

Ego provoks

The taste of victory had only fueled Suryahasa's thirst for revenge. Hemsmen, once a proud and powerful ruler of his land, now lay defeated and broken at Suryahasa's feet. But the vindictive prince was not content with mere defeat—he sought to strip Hemsmen of his dignity and make him pay for his insolence.

Suryahasa, with Hemsmen bound and silenced, took to the skies in his aircraft, the symbol of Rudraksham Kingdom adorning his captive's mouth as a grim reminder of his defeat. Their journey back to Rudraksham Kingdom became a relentless parade of punishment, an odyssey of torment that Suryahasa relished with a malevolent gleam in his eyes.

Planet after planet, universe after universe, Suryahasa made deliberate stops to exact his vengeance upon Hemsmen. Each landing became an opportunity for Suryahasa to unleash his wrath upon the fallen ruler, his fists raining blows upon the bruised and battered body. The once mighty Hemsmen was reduced to a mere puppet, a vessel for Suryahasa's sadistic desires.

On each planet they visited, witnesses trembled at the sight of Suryahasa's cruel intentions. The echoes of Hemsmen's pain reverberated through the atmosphere, a haunting testament to the lengths Suryahasa was willing to go to extract his pound of flesh. News of their macabre journey spread like wildfire, instilling fear and trepidation in the hearts of those who heard of the prince's ruthlessness.

But it was not solely Hemsmen who suffered under Suryahasa's vengeful hand. The very fabric of the universe quivered under the weight of his fury, as if the cosmos itself recoiled from the onslaught of darkness unleashed upon it. Each planet they left behind bore the scars of their presence, scarred landscapes and shattered remnants serving as a stark reminder of their destructive path.

At long last, the aircraft returned to Rudraksham Kingdom, bringing with it a battered and broken Hemsmen. Suryahasa's thirst for dominance knew no bounds, and he sought to make an example of his defeated foe. Hemsmen's broken body was suspended in the center of the kingdom's sky, a chilling display of Suryahasa's triumph and Hemsmen's humiliation.

With a vice-like grip, Suryahasa held Hemsmen by his hands, exposing him to the kingdom's gaze. The once-proud ruler, now stripped of his power and dignity, was forced to issue a public apology and beg for mercy in a voice that rang through the heavens. The somber skies absorbed Hemsmen's pleas, carrying them across the land and stirring a mix of awe, fear, and revulsion among the onlookers.

This haunting spectacle marked a turning point in the conflict between the kingdoms, leaving an indelible imprint on the collective consciousness. Suryahasa's wrath had transcended the boundaries of revenge, transforming into a chilling symbol of dominance and warning to all who dared challenge Rudraksham Kingdom's might.

As the chapter came to an end, the weight of the impending consequences hung heavy in the air. The ripples of Suryahasa's actions would not go unnoticed, for the echoes of his vengeance would reverberate throughout the realms, stoking the flames of conflict and setting the stage for a tumultuous and uncertain future.

25

Even soul begged

The atmosphere hung heavy with a mix of despair and dread as Rudraksha, the embodiment of Rudraksham Kingdom's power, issued a chilling command to Suryahasa. The torment Hemsmen had endured was to reach its horrifying climax—an act that would send shockwaves through the very fabric of existence.

Suryahasa, his face a mask of cold determination, obliged without question. Hemsmen's battered body was strapped onto the mouth of the aircraft, an eerie symbol of the prince's demise. With the weight of his final act resting heavily upon him, Suryahasa piloted the craft to the planet where the peace settlement had been planned—an unfortunate twist of fate that would forever taint the fragile hopes for reconciliation.

Above the skies where Rudraksha, Geame, Felicity, and Marfel were assigned to stay, Suryahasa positioned the aircraft, poised to unleash its devastating payload. The tension among the kingdoms was palpable, the air thick with uncertainty and apprehension. Little did they know that the gruesome spectacle about to unfold would shatter the remaining shards of peace.

With a resounding blast, Suryahasa released Hemsmen's body into the vast expanse of space. The lifeless figure careened through the celestial abyss, a haunting sight that sent shivers down the spines of all who witnessed it. In a macabre twist of fate, Hemsmen's hand, severed during the explosion, hurtled towards its own grim destination.

The hand, still adorned with the royal ring, defied the laws of gravity and found its way directly into the room where Geame and Felicity were seated. Time seemed to stand still as the ring descended into Felicity's open palm, as if guided by some unseen force. The weight of the moment was undeniable—a twisted token of Hemsmen's reign had fallen into the hands of the goddess of spirits herself.

Felicity stared at the ring, its significance not lost on her. It held within it the echoes of Hemsmen's ambition, his fall from grace, and the violence that had consumed him. The room fell into an eerie silence as all eyes turned to Felicity, anticipation and uncertainty mingling in the air.

Geame, his eyes filled with a mix of astonishment and concern, reached out to Felicity, gently taking her hand into his own. The fates had intertwined their lives in ways they could not have foreseen, and now they faced an uncertain future, where the echoes of Hemsmen's demise reverberated through their every thought and action.

In the wake of this chilling event, the seeds of war had been sown deeper, and the fragile threads of peace had unraveled further. The kingdoms stood on the precipice of an all-consuming conflict, where alliances would shift, loyalties would be tested, and the very fabric of their existence would be torn asunder.

As Chapter 24 came to a close, the implications of Hemsmen's end and the discovery of his ring in Felicity's possession set in motion a chain of events that would shape

the destiny of the kingdoms involved. The stage was now set for a clash of powers, a battle that would transcend realms and redefine the very concept of supremacy.

26

The Bloody Sky

As the brutality of Suryahasa, backed by the formidable might of Rudraksha kingdom, unfolded, a wave of terror swept through the area. The normal public, caught in the crossfire of power, screamed and scattered in panic, their voices merging with the chaos that engulfed them. But amidst the pandemonium, the kings stood still, their gaze transfixed upon a sight that would forever be etched in their memories.

Looking up to the sky, King Goister and the other kings found themselves locked in a chilling encounter. Above them, the azure expanse was adorned with a multitude of flags, all proudly bearing the emblem of Rudraksham kingdom. The symbols fluttered in the wind, a stark reminder of the kingdom's dominance and the power it wielded.

At the forefront of this haunting spectacle stood Suryahasa, a figure of indomitable strength and unwavering resolve. His presence commanded attention, radiating an aura of raw power that sent shivers down the spines of those who dared to gaze upon him. With eyes as piercing as daggers, he locked his gaze onto King Goister, as if challenging the very core of the king's being.

In that fleeting moment, a profound sense of regret washed over King Goister like an unforgiving tide. The weight of their ill-conceived decision to provoke Hemsmen in the court now bore down upon their shoulders, threatening to crush their hopes and aspirations. They had underestimated the might of Rudraksha kingdom and the consequences of their actions were laid bare before them.

Whispering to King Opel, his voice laced with a mix of apprehension and resignation, King Goister acknowledged the gravity of their mistake. The seeds of provocation they had sown had blossomed into a tempest of chaos and destruction, their hubris leading them into the very heart of the storm. Now, as they stood beneath the looming flags of Rudraksham kingdom, their resolve faltered, their confidence shaken to its core.

It was a humbling moment for both kings, a stark realization of the perils that accompany challenging powers greater than their own. They were caught in a web of their own making, entangled in a conflict that threatened to consume them all. The aftermath of their ill-fated decision unfolded before their eyes, an unfolding tapestry of fear, uncertainty, and regret.

As the chapter draws to a close, King Goister and King Opel find themselves grappling with the consequences of their actions, forced to confront the harsh reality of their choices. The specter of Rudraksha kingdom's power looms over them, casting a long shadow of doubt and trepidation. Their once-bold aspirations now hang in the balance, and the fate of their kingdoms hangs by a thread.

The story continues, the stage set for a clash of powers that will test the resilience and mettle of all involved. The reader is left eagerly anticipating the next turn of events, the looming

war that threatens to reshape the destinies of these kingdoms forever.

27

Cry Echoed

As the royal ring of Hemsmen found its way into Felicity's hand, a profound transformation took hold of her being. In that fleeting moment, her consciousness was transported to a realm beyond the tangible, a place where time and space merged into an ethereal tapestry of emotions and memories. For a few agonizing minutes, her mind ceased to function in the realm of the present.

When Felicity eventually returned to the reality of her surroundings, a torrent of emotions overwhelmed her. The weight of her loss, the void left by the absence of her beloved spouse, bore down upon her like an unbearable burden. In the depths of her grief, she crumbled, her once-resilient spirit succumbing to the weight of despair.

Tears streamed down Felicity's face, a torrential outpouring of anguish and sorrow. Each droplet carried the weight of her shattered dreams and the pain of a love cruelly snatched away. In that moment, the world around her blurred, as if mirroring the tumult within her soul.

But it was not only grief that coursed through Felicity's veins. Alongside her profound sorrow, an intense rage ignited, fueled by the injustice that had befallen her and her kingdom. It simmered within her, a tempestuous fire ready to consume everything in its path. And when she could no longer contain the storm raging within her, a scream erupted from her very core.

Her scream, so potent and raw, reverberated through the air, slicing through the silence like a blade. Its power was unfathomable, leaving all who heard it trembling in its wake. Even the youngest among them, the innocent children, found their ears robbed of sound, their world plunged into a deafening silence.

In that moment, hearts raced in synchrony, beating with a rhythm that mirrored the collective pulse of fear, grief, and awe. The sheer intensity of Felicity's cry pierced the veil of complacency, awakening a primal understanding of the pain she carried within her.

The echoes of her scream lingered in the air, a haunting reminder of the depths of human emotion and the strength that can be borne from anguish. It served as a rallying cry, a testament to the indomitable spirit that resided within Felicity and her kingdom.

As the chapter draws to a close, the aftermath of Felicity's outburst hangs heavy in the air, casting a shadow of uncertainty over the once tranquil landscape.

28
The Half of Divine Wrath

Felicity's piercing scream shattered the tranquility of the surrounding atmosphere. It echoed through the realms, resonating with a power that surpassed mortal comprehension. In that moment, the goddess of spirits within her awakened, filling her being with an otherworldly energy.

As the scream subsided, a profound stillness settled over the land. Those who had witnessed Felicity's transformation felt a shiver crawl down their spines, for they knew that something extraordinary was about to unfold. In the blink of an eye, the demure and grief-stricken widow had become a force to be reckoned with—a living embodiment of wrath and vengeance.

The very air crackled with anticipation as Felicity embraced her divine heritage. Her ethereal form radiated a potent aura that sent even the most fearsome demons cowering in fear. The power within her was ancient and boundless, transcending the boundaries of mortal limitations.

With each step, the ground quivered beneath her feet, as if paying homage to the power she possessed. Her eyes, once filled with tears, now gleamed with a divine fire. She was no longer the mourning widow, but a queen of unfathomable strength and determination.

The world watched in awe as Felicity, the goddess of spirits, prepared to unleash her wrath upon those who had dared to challenge her. The mere thought of opposing her sent shivers down the spines of even the most battle-hardened warriors. She was a living testament to the force that resided within the realm of the divine.

In the wake of Felicity's transformation, the balance of power shifted, altering the course of the impending war. The forces that had once thought themselves invincible now trembled, their bravado faltering in the face of this unforeseen threat. The battlefield was no longer defined by mortal struggles, but by the clash of godly powers.

As this chapter comes to a close, the reader is left to ponder the awe-inspiring might of Felicity, the goddess of spirits. Her unleashed fury promises a cataclysmic turn of events, forever changing the landscape of the war to come.